# The Love By Moonlight

## Series of Sweet Historical Romance

Jessica Eissfeldt

Beneath A Venetian Moon
Beside A Moonlit Shore
Jessica Eissfeldt



ISBN: 978-1-989290-06-4

**CONTAINS EXCLUSIVE BONUS CONTENT AT THE BACK:**
Meet the hero of *Beneath A Venetian Moon,* Givoanni Capriccio. PLUS! Meet the men of my Sweethearts & Jazz Nights series, set in 1940s San Francisco

# FOR A LIMITED TIME
## GET YOUR FREE SWEET ROMANCE HERE!

Get your free copy of the sweet romance *Dialing Dreams*, the first in my Sweethearts & Jazz Nights series set in 1940s San Francisco. Normally my stories are $2.99 and up, but this one is yours FREE when you download it at your favourite online retailer.

*Belinda Thompson, a telephone operator, longs to sing in the spotlight. But when Belinda puts through a fateful midnight call for Nick Hart, a broken-hearted jazz crooner who offers her a chance at her dream, will theirs be only a switchboard connection or something more, in the City by the Bay?*

## Go here to get started:

www.books2read.com/dialingdreams

## FOR A LIMITED TIME

Dear reader,

Deciding to publish these manuscripts was a risk for me.

You see, they were written years ago, when the first tentative shoots of my author career began sprouting. Before I had written anything beyond 50 pages. Before I had acquired tools, skills and practices I now utilize.

As I read back through the stories, there are places I see that could be changed or modified, thanks to the skills and abilities I've now acquired at this point in my career.

But I've chosen not to change a thing.

The thing is, as a writer, you continuously grow, change and develop. So the bar for the best story you can write always changes. For *Beneath A Venetian Moon* and *Beside A Moonlit Shore,* I sincerely believed, at the time I wrote them, they were the best stories I could write. Reading through them now, I still believe in the messages these stories convey.

So I've chosen to publish them.

With that, I humbly extend this gift of writing to you, the reader. I hope you enjoy these stories, just as they were written, all those years ago.

Happy reading,
J.E.
October 2017

P.S. – Don't forget to enjoy the exclusive BONUS CONTENT featured at the very end of this book. Meet the hero of *Beneath A Venetian Moon,* Givoanni Capriccio. PLUS! Meet the men of my Sweethearts & Jazz Nights series, set in 1940s San Francisco

# ALSO BY JESSICA EISSFELDT

*Sweet Historical Romance:*

**Sweethearts & Jazz Nights Series**
*Dialing Dreams*
*Shattered Melodies*
*Fancy Footwork*
*Unspoken Lyrics*
*The Sweethearts & Jazz Nights Series:*
*The Complete Collection*

**Love By Moonlight Series**
*Beneath A Venetian Moon*
*Beside A Moonlit Shore*
*The Love By Moonlight Series:*
*The Complete 2-Book Collection*

*Sweet Contemporary Romance*

**Prince Edward Island
Love Letters & Legends**
*This Time It's Forever*
*Now It's For Always*
*At Last It's True Love*

# Beneath A Venetian Moon

## A Novella

*#1 in the Love By Moonlight Series*

# Jessica Eissfeldt

Beneath A Venetian Moon
Jessica Eissfeldt

# Chapter One

THE MOONLIGHT SLIPPED THROUGH THE partially open window as Alessandra Velocchi smoothed her amethyst gown. If only her own escape could be so easy. But the binding ties of duty wound around her more tightly than the velvet-trimmed silver mask she wore as she stepped out of her chamber, down the stairs, and out into the waiting gondola.

She gasped as the chill waters of the Venetian canal splashed at her hem like greedy fingers trying to reclaim their prize. She shuddered, putting the childhood near-drowning experience from her mind, focusing firmly on the festivities ahead at the Doge's birthday celebration.

"Does the Contessa have an escort?" The doorman addressed Alessandra at the palace entrance.

Lifting her chin, she shook her head.

"Tonight, I am a free woman." She felt her heart swell with gladness. No father to watch her, no boring escort to hinder her. Pure, clear freedom. Just the way she liked it.

Candlelight sparkled off cut crystal chandeliers as she took a goblet of wine from a side table. Winding her way amongst mingling revelers, she spotted familiar faces all around. Laughter and accented voices drifted past her as the pull of duty pushed her to the front of the ballroom where the Doge stood.

As she approached, the Doge's ministers bowed, acknowledging her as the daughter of Venice's most powerful palace advisor.

"Before the Doge begins his own speech," stated one of the officials, "he expects to hear the address your father entrusted you with." He nodded toward Alessandra. "You have prepared?"

"Of course." As she brought her goblet to her lips to calm her nerves, a sudden shadow flickered in her peripheral vision. She glanced sideways. Now nothing. Closing her eyes for a brief second to gather her thoughts, she savored the drink's heady sweetness.

Alessandra took another sip of wine, fiddling with the stem of the goblet, watching the carved facets glimmer in the light. And again, the shadow flickered in her vision, this time closer.

She frowned. Looked around. Returned her attention to the Doge, waiting for him to give her the nod. But just then, the shadow appeared again – this time taking on a form – that of a man. With a black silk mask tied around his glossy dark hair and a velvet doublet trimmed in the same midnight shade.

This time, she openly stared at him. Watched while his furtive glances around the room displayed fear. Watched while his fluid movements wound him between guests. Watched while his steps led him closer and closer to her.

She forgot all about her staid speech as she searched the planes of his face. He was not part of the court. Or the Doge's administration. Or even a member of the Venetian aristocratic circles she'd known all her life. Though he certainly was attractive. And certainly not a boring escort. Her lips curved into a smile.

She continued to admire him, noticing that by now he stood only a few paces from her. But protocol and privilege forced her to turn away, forced her to acknowledge the Doge, who now beckoned to her.

She raised her chin and straightened her spine, pivoting to face the assemblage. As the guests' final murmurs died away, she inhaled, about to speak.

But in that brief hesitation, the masked man leapt toward her. As she startled, stepping back, her name tumbled from his lips. "Contessa Velocchi."

His eyes held hers even as he collapsed at her feet, gasping, his hand pressed to his side. And that's when she saw it. Blood. Seeping crimson onto the polished parquet floor.

She knelt, one look into that sea-green gaze telling her she had nothing to fear. Her heart filled with concern at his wound and she pulled out a handkerchief, leaning forward.

His breath warm in her ear, he whispered low, frantic. "Please...I beg of you...help me. They...want me dead."

# Chapter Two

FOR A MOMENT, SHE STARED at him, speechless. But with a quick nod, she helped him to his feet, grateful for once that her position would brook no argument.

"Apologies on behalf of my father. My...cousin...is hurt. I must tend to him."

Pressing her handkerchief to his side, Alessandra rose along with the man. The crowd did not stop her as she guided him across the ballroom, her slippered feet making no sound as the pair stepped into the marble corridor.

"You can be assured of safety with me. My father will not be back until tomorrow at sunset."

He started to speak but the skin around his mouth tightened into pain. Silently, they moved passed mullioned windows, silvery moonbeams illuminating their path.

By the time they reached the wrought-iron gates of Alessandra's home, the man's breaths came in gasps and his complexion had a deathly pallor.

She helped him into a tiny gazebo shrouded in shrubbery at the back of the property. Leaving him a moment, she returned carrying a wool blanket she placed by his side. Removing the blood-soaked handkerchief and cleansing the wound, she wiped the sweat from his brow as the leaves of the bougainvillea spangled lacy patterns on their shadowy figures.

He turned his head toward her. "Thank you – "

She smiled but laid a finger to her lips. "It's all right. Rest now. I will return at dawn." With a swirl of skirts, she left.

TRUE TO HER WORD, AS sunlight touched the tiled rooftops, Alessandra returned to the sanctuary in the back garden.

Smoothing down the front of her emerald-green day dress, she walked softly up the steps, not wanting to disturb the man.

Peering inside, she noticed spots of

blood on the crumpled wool blanket, the fabric in a heap on the painted floorboards. But no man.

Scooping up the stained blanket, her fingers encountered a sheaf of smooth, cool paper underneath. What was this? Clutching the blanket to her with one hand, she unfolded the missive with the other. And encountered three marks.

"XII?" she whispered to herself, frowning. What could it mean? It made no sense. She flipped the page over. And discovered a tiny sketch depicting the tall clock tower in St. Mark's Square. Ah. She smiled. It must be a time. And from the moon and stars hastily drawn above, it seemed to be a little past midnight. She studied the charcoal drawing further, noting two tiny figures standing at the base. One in a gown. And one in a familiar-looking doublet.

She tucked the missive into her bodice. "So he wants to meet me at the clock tower?" Her heart sped up. "But he is hurt. He cannot –"

"Who are you speaking with, Contessa?" A maid's sharp tone sliced off the rest of Alessandra's sentence.

Hugging the blanket tighter, she

turned. "No one, Maria. Now I need this cleaned. Immediately."

The maid's eyes narrowed but she bobbed acquiescence. "Right away."

THE FINAL PEAL OF THE clock tower reverberated across the canals. Midnight. Picking up her long sapphire-blue cloak, she slipped out the door, pulling her hood up to shield her face. But in so doing, she failed to notice a wavering candle flame down the hall quickly wink out.

On she hurried, starlight guiding her through the twisting, narrow streets as familiar to her as her own chambers. She turned the final corner. Out of breath, she paused, savoring the rapid pulsing of her blood in a rhythm that meant only one thing: real freedom. That sweet song of her own heart.

Swiftly traveling across the black and white tiled walkway underneath the arched colonnade, she reached their rendezvous. She peered into the blackness, moving forward.

"Signore?" she called, her voice trembling only slightly.

The faint rustle of clothing served as her sole clue to the mysterious man's whereabouts when he swept up to her.

Heat suffused her cheeks but she leaned toward him, her eyes bright. "Your mobility has improved?"

"Indeed it has. And thanks, in part, to your kind actions, Contessa." He inclined his head. "If it weren't for your very gracious aid, I fear I would not be alive this night. And so, my gratitude is yours." He sank into a deep bow and brought her hand to his lips.

'Twas all she could do to suppress a gasp. His warm, soft lips pressed against the coolness of the delicate skin on the back of her hand and drew all her focus instantly to that tiny part of her body.

She wanted to wrench her hand away. Yet she stood, frozen.

How could such a routine gesture be more intimate than the deepest of kisses? The heat of his mouth seemed a declarative statement. As if that was only the beginning of his desire for exploration.

That one point of contact between his body and hers seemed to spread through her, as if he was already kissing every inch of her, as if he meant to place the heat from his lips on every region of her body.

A sigh escaped her.

His eyes met hers, questioning and somehow answering at the same time. She wished both for his release of her hand and for the moment to last forever.

Finally, he removed his lips, leaving a circle of dampness on her skin. The cool breeze brushing against those particles of moisture felt more frigid than if he had poured seawater over her. She shivered.

He lowered her hand and straightened up. For a hair's breadth, neither spoke, both entranced by the moonlight, the night, and each other.

She was the first to break the spell, her voice uneven. "But pray tell, h-how did you know my name upon yesterday's encounter?" She crossed her arms. "What is your name? Why were you injured? And for what purpose did you impose yourself upon me in that manner?" She took a step back.

He drew in a breath. "Many in Venice speak of Conte Velocchi's beautiful daughter. And if I may confess, I had every intention of fleeing the fete last night. Moving southward – to Florence, perhaps. But," his voice was soft, sincere, "'Twas you who enchanted me."

She blushed. He continued speaking. "You see, Venice is not my homeland. I came here to hide myself from those who want me dead. Alas, they have followed and alerted those in authority here. That is the reason I was bleeding – a knife wound. And 'tis the reason I did not impose further upon your hospitality. I did not wish to bring danger to your doorstep. Because," he glanced around, "I am a wanted man."

She lifted her chin. "As you have already made clear. But you have not answered my other questions, signore."

He paused a moment, considering her before nodding. "My name is Giovanni Capriccio. I am an artist."

She cocked a brow.

"My paintings are...shall we say....controversial. At least, as deemed by the Church. They do not like them. But I, you see, I cannot help but paint what I paint."

He glanced up at the stars before look-

ing back down into her eyes. Her doubts began drifting away.

"You see." He rested a hand momentarily on his heart. "It is simply how I feel. My emotions, my feelings, my life force – all laid bare on the canvas for the world to see."

Alessandra stared back at him, eyes wide, heart pounding. What a magnificent figure he looked, there in the moonlight, his voice resonant with conviction, his eyes alight with spirit.

He flung his arms wide, his voice rising with passion. "It is not up to me what I create, but up to a greater power. A deeper force. A stronger hand than my own that guides me, leads me, shows me just the right tilt of the chin, depth of shadow, angle of lighting."

His gaze found hers again. Alessandra felt her pulse pound through her. The very essence of his being seemed to radiate through him into the cool night air, into her pores, into her heart, into her soul.

And before she could think twice, she had closed the space between them, moving noiselessly in her satin slippers to stand on tiptoe and brush her lips against his, watching surprise flicker in his eyes. But he soon relented, wrapping his arms around her waist. The warm moist softness of the kiss pulled them under as he drew her even nearer while she reached a hand up to twine her fingers through his smooth dark hair.

"I had to risk it," he murmured against her mouth. "That's why I asked you here tonight. I want to paint you. And for that privilege, I would chance it all."

⋙⋘

"WHAT IS THIS?" ALESSANDRA'S FATHER demanded, indicating the blood-spattered handkerchief.

Alessandra lifted her chin. "I pricked myself while sewing. It is nothing."

"That is not what Maria said. She also said she saw you run off at nightfall yesterday."

Alessandra's cheeks flamed but she tightened her jaw. "Father. You have no right to watch me thus. I am, after all, almost –"

He cut her off with a gesture. "No, daughter, I have every right. While you live under this roof, you obey me. Especially since I have been informed a dangerous heretical traitor lurks in the byways." He glared down at her. "As you full well know, it is the sworn duty of my station…"

Alessandra bowed her head.

"I need not continue." Relenting, he placed a hand on her shoulder. "Dearest, you must know that I do this only with your safety in mind." His voice softened, dropped. "You know how it has been since your mother died." He sighed heavily and stroked her hair. "I do love you, sweet one."

She flinched. Did he, truly? She studied her toes, remembering that terrible day. "Yes, Father." Her chin trembled and she hugged him, the embrace pushing away those dark thoughts. "I know." The warmth enveloped both of them, and Alessandra felt a tear slide down her cheek.

"Daughter." Her father spoke into her hair. "Promise me you will not leave this house after nightfall unescorted."

She took a deep breath, inhaling his familiar scent – cardamom and tobacco. Her father was right. He was only doing this out of love. How could she disobey?

The jacquard of his vest smooth against her cheek, she nodded her assent, though her heart squeezed when Giovanni's face, seen so often in her daydreams of late, flashed through her mind. "I promise."

PAUSING ALONG THE RIALTO'S OUTER steps the following week as the sun hovered low over the Aegean, Alessandra stared out into the serene waters, seeing not the glasslike surface but instead a pair of soulful green eyes. "Giovanni," she whispered aloud, then covered her mouth with a quick hand as she glanced around.

Passersby, though, did not turn their heads toward her nor stop to linger at the view. Instead, they headed home, or to market, their footsteps measured and deliberate. Street urchins, begging for coins, sat at the foot of the bridge, eyes bright when the rattle of silver filled their cups.

Her mind wandered again. What sort of paintings did he paint? What made them so formidable? Why had he said he wanted to paint her last week, and then vanish?

Had he been caught, then? Her stomach clenched at the thought. Was she really that naïve to have believed him?

She wound a strand of hair around her finger as she frowned down at the water again. Not only that, what had possessed her to kiss him? Conte Velocchi's daughter should not conduct herself in such a manner. Yet she had. Her lips twisted. What had she been thinking?

With a last glance at the fading glory of the sunset, she turned and began to move down the staircase, mindful of her promise to her father and of the lengthening shadows signaling twilight's approach.

But a tug on her skirts interrupted her progress. A ragged boy stood looking up at her, holding out a tightly folded piece of paper. "Por chi," he said, his gaze darting to and fro. "Tonight."

Her fingers shook as she dropped a single gold florin into the boy's hand. "Grazie."

She hurried onward toward home, went inside and pulled out the paper only after she fled up the stairs and shut the door of her chambers. By the light of a flickering candle she hastily lit in the safety of her boudoir, she unfolded the parchment. Her eyes widened. She studied the sketch. Done in rapid strokes, the lines captured her profile perfectly as she had contemplated the canal waters only hours before. And in tiny writing, scrawled near the bottom, she read: "25 Via Ghirladio."

It must be the address of his studio. Or at least where he was hiding. Was it safe, though, to go? She inspected the picture again. How could she betray her father? After all he'd been through? Then again, he had betrayed her.

She bit her lip and put aside the paper, picking up her hairbrush. Her knuckles whitened as her fingers closed around the ivory handle. Alessandra's secret – and last remaining – reminder of her mother. The only remnant her father hadn't destroyed.

Brushing her hair in long, even strokes, she studied her own reflection. The very image of her father, down to the softly curling blond hair, the caramel-brown eyes, the pale complexion. And the stubborn chin. She reached a fingertip out to trace the looking glass. No, she could not get away from him, even here.

Recollection brought a smile to her

lips, though. The stubborn chin. Her mother had liked to call it resolve, but it had gotten Alessandra into more than one predicament.

But this wasn't a predicament. This was adventure. Intrigue. And perhaps – her heart thudded – payback. For when Father had shown up too late. Too late to save her mother. Her chest tightened. And almost too late to save her.

Though Father might not understand, or approve, how could she betray her own heart? 'Twas the sole piece of freedom she had left to call her own.

Decision made, she snuffed out the candle. With stiff fingers, she secured her now-plaited hair with a satin ribbon. Pulling her embroidered silk dressing gown around her, she watched the moon rise and the stars spread their glitter through the heavens.

Satisfied she could escape undetected, she slipped over the threshold of her room out into the corridor and shut the heavy oak door with a soft click. She wended her way down the stairs and out into the night.

# Chapter Three

THE ROOM WAS AWASH IN candlelight, every flat surface covered with tiny wax columns flickering gold at the tips. From the easel propped in the corner to the shuttered window ledges. Even the scarred floorboards bore the hot spattering of dripping wax. Alessandra blinked in awe at the golden glow. "It's magnificent. But how can you have all of this here when you are in hiding?"

Giovanni smiled. "A good friend of mine lives below these eaves during the long days of summer. I have used this space in years past."

She could see the warm invitation in his eyes. But her father's voice echoing through her mind made her duck her head, clutching her cloak more tightly around her. She glanced at him, wary, as she stood on the threshold of the room.

She did not know him, reason told her. She did not have cause to trust him, logic said. Yet her heart whispered, step forward. And so she did.

"Please, make yourself comfortable." Giovanni indicated the pile of plump silken cushions in the corner across from his easel, their hues of magenta, cobalt and emerald inviting repose.

She crossed to the pillows and sank into their softness. "I've never sat for a portrait before," Alessandra confessed. "At least, not my own. Father had a family portrait done..." Pain flitted across Alessandra's features. "When my mother was still alive."

Giovanni picked up his charcoal. "I am truly sorry for your loss," he murmured, his green eyes compassionate.

"Our only painting." She felt a spark of malcontent ignite at the memory.

He spoke softly. "She is always with you, in that portrait. 'Tis fortunate."

"No. 'Tis not." Though embers of anger glowed hot, her voice did not rise beyond a whisper. "Father abhors art."

"Why?"

She blinked at him in disbelief. He

wanted to understand her? She felt tears blur her vision. To empathize with her? She placed a trembling hand over her heart. Unlike Father, who only expected duty. Unlike the aristocratic circles that dwelled in gossip and artiface. He seemed to genuinely acknowledge her. To want her to speak her truth.

"After..." She took a deep breath. "After Mother died, he could not bring himself to look at our painting. It haunted him, he said, reminding him of the devils of his conscience that screamed at him." Swallowing, she continued in a low voice. "Because he'd killed her. He arrived too late to save her."

"From what?" Giovanni asked gently.

Alessandra looked up at him, eyes wide. "Drowning." A shudder passed through her. She closed her eyes briefly. "Which is why you are in even graver danger. For if my father, who is head of the committee to find the heretic, were to find out what we were doing, all the angels in heaven could not save you, I fear."

"Do not worry, m'lady. He shall know nothing of this collaboration."

She studied his confidence as he stud-

ied the canvas. Finally, he said, "Turn your head a little to the right."

Alessandra complied, the light from the candles soothing her, calming her fears and filling her heart with reassurance and gladness. Yes, she decided, she'd done exactly the right thing in coming here. No matter what tomorrow brought. Enjoying this moment, however brief, however fleeting, was most important. To live each moment as if it was the very last, she decided. And therefore, her father's warnings and actions were of no consequence. Her heart knew the truth. And the truth was –

She startled out of her reverie when the floorboards creaked. Giovanni, wiping charcoal off his fingers with a rag, cleared his throat. "If I may make an adjustment?"

Though her heart fluttered in her chest, her voice remained steady. "Do what you must. You are, after all, the artist."

He approached, hesitating only a moment before sinking to his knees beside her. His body heat radiated toward her as he extended a hand. She met his gaze levelly, seeing a concentrated yet creative and curious light in his eyes.

His fingers brushed, firm and warm, against her chin, gently tilting her head so that the shadow previously created was now bathed in luminescence.

Before she could take a breath, his fingertips grazed her collarbone, smoothing out the delicate silk of her dressing gown so that it draped in soft folds against the creaminess of her now-exposed shoulder.

The only sound in the small space was the slow rhythm of their breathing as they stared at each other. She saw the glow in his eyes' green depths and knew that glow mirrored her own expression. Warmth spread through her, surging powerfully through her veins. But she was not frightened of that power, she realized, as she reached out to wipe away a paint fleck from his jawline. It simply served to strengthen her. She straightened her spine, smiled at him. He smiled back, placing his hand over hers where it rested on his face. He raised her fingertips to his lips and gave her hand a gentle squeeze before releasing it and returning to his canvas.

He loaded the brush and began working once more, a deep furrow of concentration marring the expanse of his forehead. She longed to smooth the frown away, to make the creation process easy and effortless for him.

She watched as the candles guttered, pools of wax growing larger and larger. But Giovanni simply continued working, oblivious to anything but his canvas.

She shifted on the cushions. Had she surmised wrongly? Was it only the painting he cared about? Was he only using her for his art? She looked at him as he frowned at the canvas, his head cocked as he examined his work.

He paused to roll up his sleeves, not heeding the paint splatters that now covered his muslin shirt. Mixing cyan and cerulean, he began dabbing the canvas again. Long minutes passed in silence.

No. She shook away the traitorous thoughts. She had no reason to doubt him, or herself. She recalled that deep warmth in his expression, that sincerity of his tone as he explained his art to her, as he told her he wanted to paint her.

He looked up from the easel at last. "This evening's session is almost complete. I need only a few moments more before you are free to go."

Free to go. His words sent a chill through her that did not correlate to the cold draft that had worked its way through a crack in the garret wall. She did not want to be free of him – she tugged the thin cotton of her nightgown and the thicker silk of her dressing gown around her as the shock of realization set in – she did not want to leave his side.

But she didn't have that freedom. Not now. Not ever. Not as long she shared a roof with Father. She felt her heart constrict, her fists tighten at her sides. An ache blazed in her soul. "Though you are running from so many, you are so free."

He put down his brush. Came to her once more. Took her hands and held them between his, his voice low, soft. "My uncle, a dignitary in Verona, displayed my very first painting in the hallway of his home. A member of the clergy saw the painting. So taken with it, the man realized I would be the perfect painter for his refectory hall. One fresco led to another. My reputation grew, spreading through the country-side. 'Twas more than I had hoped. Miraculous, truly." He bowed his head.

"But," he frowned, "the more frescoes I painted the more dissatisfied I became. It felt too restricting. Too confining. But I ignored that feeling. Until one day, I was painting a religious scene for a Catholic church in Verona. Angels, demons, saints and sinners. But I just could not make them so stiff and so wooden. It felt like a tragedy." He pressed a hand to his heart. "As I was working, lost in concentration, my brush simply took on a life of its own. Infusing the painting with vibrancy, with movement. I created it in my own style. My own way. The entire painting." He whispered fiercely. "And I did not regret it one bit." He stopped, eyes alight, gaze locked with Alessandra's. "Not one bit."

A shiver of hope trembled through Alessandra.

"And that is why," he finished, "they pursue me. That is why they want to be rid of me. My paintings," he inhaled, "frighten the magistrates with the breath of life they convey."

Alessandra remained wordless.

He blinked, exhaling slowly. "May I show you something?" He extended his hand, inclining his head. She rose, placing her palm against his.

Guiding her gently, he led her to a corner where several blank canvases leaned against the wall. "Pick one."

Delight leapt into her eyes. She raised a finger to the white expanse, imagining vivid colors varnished on the surface. "You are a creator of dreams." She swallowed. "Magic and brilliance and beauty." Turning away, she wiped at her eyes with the edge of her lace handkerchief. "How I wish I could have some of that."

"Contessa." He laid a hand on her elbow. "You do. Everyone," he whispered, putting a supportive arm around her waist, "does."

He smoothed a stray tendril off her forehead. "Why do you think otherwise?"

She rested her head against his chest. And laughed without mirth. "In my world, nothing is said without thinking. Every rule is observed. No brilliance. No magic. Just duty and protocol. Until now." She pushed away from him. "Until your words pressed against this floodgate within." She spun to face him. "I want to be free of this burden."

"You can be free," he whispered, carrying the canvas she had chosen to his easel.

He handed her the palette. "I will show you how." He put his paintbrush in her fingers. "Close your eyes," he murmured, his lips next to her ear. "Do not think. Simply feel. That pain, that ache you have within you? Draw from it. Use it. Take it," he guided her hand to the canvas, "and create."

For many moments, she stood at the easel, fingers trembling, eyelids fluttering. She gripped the paintbrush so tightly her knuckles were white.

"Let go," Giovanni encouraged. "You are simply the channel for creation. It will flow if you allow it."

Nodding, she loosened her grip, inhaled and closed her eyes once again. Slowly at first, then gradually with more fluidity, the brush moved in Alessandra's hand, side to side, back and forth.

The faintest quiver of a smile began to form on her lips as her brushstrokes grew more confident. Bolder. Leaving bright trails of reds, blues and yellow, splatters and drips unheeded as she dipped again and again into that deep well within that had been sealed shut for so long.

Her brush moved faster and faster and her smile grew larger and larger. A laugh of delight escaped her. Then another. Waves of giddy joy surged through her as she lost herself in the moment, carrying every last vestige of repressed feeling onto the canvas until finally she stopped, chest heaving, body swaying.

She opened her eyes. Seeing the splashes of color, seeing all her emotions transferred from within her onto the canvas, her soul bright, fresh and clean, she sprang toward Giovanni, throwing her arms wide and embracing him.

"Thank you," she cried, "thank you, thank you." She dropped kisses across his forehead, cheekbones, lips.

His arms encircled her waist. "It is a great day when one is handed the keys to one's own freedom." He stroked her cheek, admiration and respect shining in his eyes. "I am so pleased for you.

"But," he said with a reluctant sigh, releasing her, "we must return to work. I have only a few more touches before tonight's work is complete." He indicated the cushions.

And so it went. Every evening. For a

full fortnight. She continued to sit. And he continued to paint. Until the low gong of St. Mark's cathedral bells could be heard ringing in the dawn.

Those dulcet tones broke the enchantment each evening, propelling Alessandra to her feet. She was at the room's threshold, her hand on the latch. But tonight was different.

"The painting is finally done. It shall be delivered at nightfall." Giovanni gave a deep bow. "You have my word." He crossed the room to her, resting a hand briefly on the small of her back before sealing his promise with the warm sweetness of a kiss.

"WHAT IS TROUBLING YOU, MY sweet?" Conte Velocchi pushed aside his pewter dinner plate, the remains of a game hen strewn on its surface. He leaned across the fine linen tablecloth, concern in his eyes.

"Nothing, Father." Alessandra clutched her fork, took a breath and rearranged her expression into one of calm, though an ocean of torment raged inside her. Where was he? It had been almost one whole day already and no word from him. Her eyes sought the clock on the mantelpiece. Three more hours and he would officially have broken his word to her. Did all those nights spent together mean nothing?

She swallowed, shoving aside her own plate, its contents untouched. "I am going to retire for the evening. Please, have no one disturb me."

Conte Velocchi frowned, but nodded to his daughter. "As you wish."

With the door safely shut behind her, Alessandra began pacing, her slippers scuffing slightly against the rough, uneven stone. She would not look at the mantel, she would not. But her eyes betrayed her and strayed to the tiny hour hand anyway. Oh, how foolish she had been, trusting a stranger, throwing herself without thought at him. Going to his studio so many times, posing for him, sharing secrets, joys, hopes – all with him. How utterly ridiculous. She flung herself across her bed with a sigh, sinking into the eiderdown duvet, staring up at the ceiling's elaborate crown molding edged in gilt. His green eyes seemed to dance before her, the memory of his lips fused with hers too much to bear.

She wiped away a trickle of wetness from her cheek, clenching her jaw. She would not allow herself this mood. She lifted her chin. If he said he would come, he would. And if he did not, well, certainly that was not her fault.

Pushing herself up, she moved to the casement, throwing open the shutters and breathing deeply of the night air, its coolness soothing her flaming cheeks. She leaned further out, admiring the tiny diamond pinpricks of light, searching for her favorite constellation, Cassiopeia. Ah, there she was. Sitting proudly on her throne.

The wind picked up, whispering its way around the corners and cervices of the slumbering city, lulling her with its rhythms. Toying with her loosened tresses. Seeming to whisper her name. *Alessandra.* Almost as if he was speaking to her. *Alessandra.* Calling out to her.

"Alessandra." Yes, there it was again. Only, only...it wasn't the wind at all. It was him. She heard her name again from below and when she looked down, she saw him, his eyes gleaming the moonlight, an oblong package under his arm.

Elation filled her. "Stay a moment. I shall come down."

Unheeding of anything but her own joy, she fairly flew through the house, out the front door and down into the court-yard. She eased open the heavy wrought-iron gate, its weight grating against the cobblestones. She winced and glanced around – too late to see a candle flame extinguish from her father's study.

She had just squeezed through the small opening when Giovanni appeared before her, sweeping into a low bow.

But her elation died, replaced by hor-ror. For his grandiose entrance could not hide the ripped fabric of his tunic, the smear of dirt and blood across his cheek-bone or the raggedness of his inhalations and exhalations. He rose from the bow, wobbling a moment before holding out the rolled canvas.

Without a word, she grasped his hand, guiding him into the deeper shadows, the soft splashing of the fountain in the center of the courtyard the only backdrop of sound as she sank onto a small stone

bench.

He, however, remained standing. "I fear I cannot tarry."

"We shall be sheltered here."

"Alessandra...I do not wish to endanger you further." His voice lowered and he took a step forward. "But I knew I would never forgive myself if I broke my sworn oath to you. And so, I came. Nay." He knelt before her. "I could not stay away. I had to see the expression on your face..." He reached out to trace the outline of her jaw with a fingertip. "When I brought you – this."

She held her breath as he untied the string securing the canvas, watched as he deftly unrolled his masterpiece.

And it was undeniably so. She gasped as she studied the painting. No mistaking it was her. But the fluid, flowing, graceful creature that stared back at her in a swirl of purples, blues and violets, the colors seeming to blend together, lift up and almost vibrate with life and energy, surely, surely, that could not be her? But it was. She sucked in her breath. Indeed, 'twas her very essence. The deepest core of her soul. And he had perfectly portrayed it there, for the world to see. For her.

Wordless, she embraced him. Gratitude and love pulsed through her as she felt his arms slide around her, felt his warm hands gently hold her, felt his heart open to hers, felt their souls entwine. And in that moment, she knew.

She felt his arms tighten around her in response. He knew it too, she realized. The night cloaked them both – a solemn, silent witness to their whispered exchange of eternal promise to each other.

But that sweet promise tasted ashen as she noticed water droplets splashing onto the fountain's marble edge, half-covered by the shifting shadows of the leafy bougainvillea so close to the gazebo – the scene of their first transgression. And all at once, fear burst into flame inside her heart. It was too late. Too late. He knew, she realized. Father knew.

The dull thud of leather boots on cobblestones rang out like cannon fire, ricocheting them apart before she could utter warning.

"You." Her father's tone, low, menacing, filled her with sick dread. And an anger of her own.

He swiftly crossed the courtyard, his eyes burning with fury, his hand reaching for the hilt of his dagger.

She whirled, stepping into his path even as Giovanni stood by her side, reaching for his own weapon. A flash of silver alerted Alessandra to the small blade Giovanni unsheathed with trembling fingers. He had nowhere to run.

"Baleful coward. Stand away from my daughter," Conte Velocchi snarled, moving to push Alessandra aside.

But she stood firm. "How dare you treat me – us – thusly! We are not pawns in one of your precious chess matches. And I – I am your own flesh and blood!"

"Oh, daughter, you –"

But seeing the painting half unfurled on the stone bench, the conte lunged toward it, holding it aloft in the faint starlight. Before Alessandra could stop him, he'd rent the painting in half, his eyes blazing.

A choked cry came from Giovanni. He leapt toward Alessandra's father, slicing open the raw silk of the conte's sleeve, his dagger leaving slashes of red on the older man's skin. "You dare to desecrate my masterpiece!" The artist's blade flashed again – this time, a crimson crescent burst angrily across the conte's jaw.

"Heretic," Conte Velocchi bellowed, moving in to retaliate. "Traitorous betrayer. You shall pay for all of your sins – with your life."

Droplets of blood dripped like tears onto the cold stone, the pale gleam of moonlight reflected in the scarlet pooling. Sadness seeped into Alessandra as she watched their struggle.

Giovanni, in his haste to be away, tripped over their small stone bench. With a cry, he landed hard, the air knocked out of him.

Alessandra held her own breath, feeling a whisper of night air brush by her, carrying the dewy scent of summer roses. But their perfume did nothing to mask the stench of fear that hovered between the two men and clung to each breath of breeze as it fanned her cheek. Fear of love – and fear of despair.

Though dazed, Giovanni scrabbled for his dropped weapon. But he was too slow and Conte Velocchi lunged. Wrenching Giovanni's arms behind him, the conte dragged him out into the center of the

courtyard.

"Father!" Alessandra cried out. "You cannot do this." She flew toward her father again, trying in vain to pry the conte's fingers loose from Giovanni's arm. "He has done nothing wrong. Nothing!"

"Silence, daughter. I must. For it is my God-given duty to do so. He must pay for his traitorous ways." He shook Giovanni, who, weaponless, struggled against the older man's heavily muscled bulk. The conte, teeth clenched, pressed his blade to the artist's throat. "Works of his demonic hand bring the Old Masters' holy art to shame. These blasphemous canvases must be destroyed. And the painter with them. It would be a sin not to."

Bringing the butt of the weapon to Giovanni's skull, the conte's roared oath drowned out Alessandra's scream.

"And you, daughter..." The full force of the conte's wrath vibrated through her. "Do not dare go against me. For I shall disown you if you do."

As he dragged Giovanni's limp form away, she sank to the ground, reaching for the now-destroyed painting that lay soiled and crushed in the darkness, its torn edges fluttering helplessly in the breeze.

"No," she uttered in a strangled whisper, her pent-up tears now falling hot and fast on the shredded surface, creating pools of dark on what had once been a treasure so full of bright-hearted hope and love.

# Chapter Four

ALESSANDRA, PRONE ON HER BED, watched, listless, as the lone candle on her bedside table sputtered once, twice, and then went out. She wiped away a fresh trail of tears. She would never see him again. Never. Oh, how petty and trivial her concerns of last night had seemed, when she had simply wondered if he would come. How naïve.

A knife of pain sliced at her heart. Now he would die. Because of her. And she could do nothing for him. Nothing. Even less than nothing, now that Father had alerted the ministers, who had immediately sentenced his execution for the morrow's dawn. And the conte had forbidden her exit from her chambers. She balled her hands into fists as helplessness washed through her.

Unable to lie down any longer, she

sprang up, pacing back and forth by the window in her bare feet, unheeding the cold leaching into her bones as she wildly strode to and fro. There had to be something she could do, something. Anything. She scrubbed away more tears. They seemed to fall endlessly.

She wanted to scream, throw herself onto the cold ground. Wanted to hurt her father as much as he had hurt her. How could he betray her thus? She loved him. She crumpled to the ground as more sobs wracked her. And why was she forced to make a choice between the two men she loved? Why? What cruel fate had enacted this outcome?

She knew not how long she crouched on the flagstones, rending open her wounded soul with a frenzy of fresh pain.

But as the grey light of morning crept through the heavy velvet drapes, the seeds of a plan nudged at her heart. She slowly exhaled. Would that possibly work? She cocked her head, mulling it over. Perhaps. The tiniest particle of hope sprouted within her. She wiped her cheeks dry.

Getting up, she checked the door once more, giving it a firm rattle to ensure it was

still locked. She stooped, pressing her ear to the keyhole and holding her breath. Nothing stirred.

Crossing to the armoire, she unlocked one of the walnut paneled doors with a deft flick of her wrist. Plucking out her oldest, plainest dress, she pulled it on. Tucking her hair up into a kerchief, she surveyed herself in the looking glass. She frowned. Not quite complete.

Bending over the ashes of the now-dead fire in the hearth, she smudged her forehead and cheeks with soot, running her soiled fingers across the front of her skirt and bodice. Turning back to the mirror, she smiled in satisfaction. A red-eyed serving girl looked back at her.

Heading to the casement, she flung open the shutters and secured them to the window ledge, then leaned out. Though her window was only one level above the street, she felt her resolve slipping. But the memory of Giovanni's arms around her solidified her determination once more. She eased over the edge of the window.

HER HEART HAMMERED IN HER chest but she tightened her jaw, her head bowed. No one spared her an additional glance when she stepped into the shadow of the palace's back entrance. Blending in with the other members of the working class up at dawn to clean, scrub and serve, she kept her eyes trained on the cobblestones.

Each step on the cold stone built her confidence. She would find him. A sudden bubble of happiness formed in her chest. Strength expanded it until it shimmered through her. She would make everything all right again. They would be together.

All at once, a foul-smelling wooden bucket was thrust under her nose and an angry voice blasted in her ear. "You – girl! Get yourself to work."

Alessandra darted a glance in the direction of the words. A scowling heavyset woman frowned down at her, hands on hips. "Are you deaf as well as mute? Conchetta's replacement is stupider than she was. Pah!" The woman spat. "The prisoners do not take out their own slop. Go!"

A hard shove sent Alessandra reeling through a rough-hewn doorway. Clutching

the bucket's frayed rope handle, its fibers scratching her palm, Alessandra wended her way through a maze of stairways and long corridors.

Somewhere in the sprawling opulence lay the connecting door to the prison where Giovanni languished. But where, oh where was that hideous place?

Wandering down another, narrower corridor, trying not to sink into the despair that wanted to assail her, she almost tripped in the dim light over a waiflike slip of a girl. Clad in a dirty frock much like Alessandra's, she knelt on the floor, scrubbing the ancient stones. The girl looked up, meeting Alessandra's gaze. Dull apathy met shocked surprise.

"Excuse me, miss. I did not see you there."

The girl gave a shrug, about to return her attention to the floor, when Alessandra touched her lightly on the shoulder, kneeling down to look into her eyes.

Holding up her wooden bucket, Alessandra indicated the hall. "The prison?"

The girl simply pointed to a small door shrouded in shadow. Alessandra squinted. It sat at the top of a set of stairs that fronted the end of the corridor they occupied.

Opening her mouth to politely say thank you, she shut it again when she remembered she was supposed to be a servant as well. She simply nodded. The girl went back to scrubbing.

LOW MOANS AND MUFFLED GROANS fell on her ears long before the door's hinges creaked open. And the smells. Alessandra gagged, bringing the sleeve of her gown to her nose, trying to avoid the putrid odors. Though her stomach roiled, she forced her feet forward, knowing that now, at last, she was almost to her beloved. How she would get him out, though, would be another matter, she decided, best be solved at the time.

Crouching to fit herself into the narrow, low-hung doorway, the rough voice of the guard growled at her. "Going somewhere, missy?"

She held up her bucket.

He grunted, jerking his head sideways, indicating she could pass, eyeing suspi-

ciously the bit of finely wrought lace that peeked from her hem.

Resisting the urge to flinch away from him, she stepped into the claustrophobic, hand-hewn stone aisleway, iron-barred doors extending in long succession before her. She swallowed. Slop duties, she realized, meant just that. But she set her mouth and continued to each cell's chamber pot. Beads of sweat rolled down her face, strands of hair sticking damply to her cheeks and neck.

Using the opportunity, though, to ascertain the identity of each prisoner she saw, she soon realized Giovanni was not among them. Hope rippled through her.

Until it died again at the final cell. For there, framed between the bars, was Giovanni, prone on the straw pallet in the far corner.

Her heart sped up and her hands shook as she reached for the chamber pot placed outside the door. She dared a low whisper. "Giovanni." No movement. She tried again, calling a bit louder. Still no answer.

She bit her lip, felt her chin begin to quiver. She had failed him. She turned away, clenching the bucket so tightly her nails cut into her palm, her head lowered.

But what was that? A faint rustle of movement. She froze. Dropped the bucket with a thud. Whirled around, pressing herself against the locked door's impenetrable mass.

"I am so very sorry," she sobbed.

He slowly sat up, his voice bravely gentle. "Do not apologize, for you are not at fault. The creativity that brought that painting to life never dies, my love. It never dies."

He climbed to his feet and she watched with awe as that impassioned light came into his eyes. "It is the very air we breathe." He came to the grate across the door, wrapping his fingers around the iron bars. "It is the miracles and marvels we witness every day." His gaze burned into hers. "Though that painting might be gone, our love still exists. Our love will always remain. Always. No one," he whispered fiercely, "can destroy that."

Breathless, she managed, "I will get you out of this dreadful place."

"My love..." His tone betrayed a tremor of fear. "There is..." His voice broke. "...no way." He raked a hand through his hair.

"Though I have tried."

"There is," she insisted, panic lacing its way through her, quickly followed by anger. "There has to be." Her eyes flashed. And suddenly, means to his escape came to her. The guard. Of course. She approached him, bobbing a curtsy, forcing her genteel accent into a guttural tone. "The final prisoner, sir, he does not stir."

"Then leave him for dead," the guard snarled, glaring at her.

"But sir," she protested, holding up her bucket. "His – "

"I said, leave him! He's set to hang at dawn. And what is it to you?" He gave her a long look. "Lovers?" He snorted with contempt as she glanced back down to the final cell. "Serves you right." Before she could do anything else, he cuffed her on the cheek. "Get out, wench, before I throw you in one of these cells myself."

Pain sparked across her cheekbone. Legs quaking, lips trembling, she stumbled, tripping over the threshold, spilling the contents of the bucket all down her skirt.

SHE KNEW NOTHING BUT THE sting of failure and the bitter tang of disappointment mixed with regret and salted with the grief of her tears as she ran blindly down back alleys and across courtyards. Her chest tightened and a cry of anguish ripped through her. She had failed him.

Unheeding of where her footfalls landed, she did not see the rain-dark puddle along the waterway's edge. Splashing into the shallow pool, she slipped. Swaying first one way and then the other, she came dangerously close to the canal's edge. A torrent of image-laced sensations flooded her.

Terror. Freezing blackness. White. White hands. Whites of her mother's eyes widening...widening...then filling with tears. Fingers clutching – spasmodic. Choking. Gasping. Cold, so cold. Overwhelming her. Pulling her down, down, down into those swirling eddies of the past.

Her feet scrabbled, seeking purchase on the slippery stone, her arms pinwheeling. But the seemingly serene surface lapping against boat hulls and slapping against moorings simply waited – indifferent to her fate.

The flurry of a mourning dove's wings, spreading white and pure against the waning moon, captured her periphery. Hope. Life. Pulling her out of the past. Her muscles tensed and strained until finally, finally, she had righted herself.

Though panting and shaken, she pushed onward, finally drawing to a halt at her father's doorway. Her eyes darted to her darkened window. Too late, she realized her mistake. She couldn't climb back up there. Nor could she use the servants' entrance without being seen at this hour. She had no choice but to knock and give herself away. All for naught. And what of her father's words? A tremor passed through her. Would he truly throw her out onto the streets?

Inhaling, she raised her chin. Lifting the knocker, she sounded out her certain doom. Maria answered, her eyes widening then narrowing. "I shall have to call your father. At once."

Though exhaustion caused Alessandra to sway on her feet, she contemplated dashing up the wide staircase and into the haven of her chambers. But before she could put action to thought, her father bore down on her, his expression steely.

He said nothing, simply taking her arm, his fingers vise-like. He pulled her inside and down the hall to his study. Releasing her, she stumbled to a chair, her heart jumping against her ribs like a frightened hare.

But still he did not speak, simply stared into the fireplace flames for a long moment, his jaw clenching and unclenching. Suddenly, he wheeled, his tone a low utterance. "You dare disobey me." His eyes narrowed. "I told you – I told you, daughter. That man – " He gave a mirthless laugh, slamming a hand down onto his mahogany writing desk. "Is a criminal. Worse, a heretic. And what did you do? Put yourself right in his path." He leaned toward her. "Right. In. His. Path." His eyes flashed fire. "I tried to protect you. For your own good, daughter. Your own good." He shook his head. "But now, you need to know the price of sacrifice. The price of –"

"But Father!" She jumped up, a frisson of energetic indignation surging through her. "I love him! None of those other things matter. Our love is...We are...." She dashed drops from her cheeks.

"Alessandra." His voice softened at her sadness. "It cannot be. You brought dishonor upon this house, upon me, and worse, upon yourself and your own reputation. No one will ever look at you again, much less ask me for your hand."

"There is no one else I want besides Giovanni." She spread her arms wide. "No one – "

In the refracted firelight, Alessandra caught the regret and sadness in her father's eyes. "It is not about want, but about duty. And it is too late." He sighed, the anger replaced by stone-cold resolve. "You must learn that your impulsive choices have consequences. That your actions bring repercussions not only upon yourself but also on those around you."

Alessandra's last flutterings of hope died at her father's tone. She could only await his next words with what shred of pride she still possessed.

"Thus, though it pains me," he lowered his voice, "you shall leave this household. At once."

Alessandra let out a cry of dismay. "Please! I beg of you, on Mother's life, to –"

"Do not speak of your mother to me." And he turned his back to her.

# Chapter Five

THOUGH HER SOILED GOWN CHAFED painfully, it seemed a gentle mercy compared to the weight Alessandra carried within her heart. She rubbed her cold feet together, shivering in the predawn dark in St. Mark's Square as she stood along the edge of the canal, just to the left of the gallows by the clock tower. She watched a flock of pigeons peck, oblivious to death's doorway so near.

Her eyes strayed back to the clock tower. Their rendezvous. How long ago it now seemed – a fleeting warm flame in the endless night that her life had become. How would she be able to survive without Giovanni? Or her own father? Oh, she had thought she wanted freedom. And it had come to her, she realized now. Indeed it had. Her father had seen to that. She hung her head, too full of remorse to feel anger.

Her mind drifted back to Giovanni and she sighed. What heights of freedom her heart knew when encircled by his arms. Crystalline, clear. He had not captured her heart, dragging it down, but instead sent it soaring. Rising higher than she'd ever dreamt possible – allowing her the expansive possibilities of becoming more fully herself. Love did not entrap, but put on wings.

Wings that had been singed, charred, blackened beyond recognition. Terror trickled through her veins, its iron manacles caging her heart and entrapping her spirit. For this, this, was not freedom at all. Not now. Not without Giovanni. Not if her father had his way, she thought, her mouth tightening. Would any flights of fancy, never mind life itself, ever be sweet again if she could not give life and breath to this love in her heart, if she could not find a dear repository for this overflow of affection, attention, passion?

A rough voice called, "Make way for the prisoners," jarring her out of the agony of her mind and into the torture of her present. She raised her head. Bodies jostled as a pathway parted, the prisoners, she realized, trooping past right in front of her. And then she saw him. The final prisoner in the row of doomed men.

Her heart leapt, the searing pain of the previous hours washed away by the sight of him coming ever closer to her. Nearer and nearer until he was a mere step away, nothing between them – except everything they couldn't have prevented.

Even at this hour of darkness, his green eyes, burning bright with the fierce pride he harbored in his soul and the deep love in his heart, found and held hers. "Alessandra!" He stretched out his hands, struggling against the ropes binding his wrists.

She reached for him, her face wet. Raising trembling fingers straining to intertwine with his, she poured every sweet love-word, every dear love-thought, into each syllable of his name. "Giovanni!"

The people around them muttered impatiently, pushing and shoving. Alessandra stumbled, and their hands wrenched apart. Now perilously close to the open water, Alessandra caught her balance with a gasp. Giovanni held her gaze as long as he could, an "I love you" torn from his lips as

he was pushed toward the scaffolding steps. The guard, sniggering, gave him a hard shove. "Move along, move along."

She brought her lace handkerchief to her face, choking back a sob as she squeezed her eyes shut. But her senses could not be stifled. The salty breeze from the canal curled around the nape of her neck, its dampness taunting her, sending a shiver coursing down her spine, filling her head once more with those half-buried memories.

Alessandra glanced once, twice, at the blue-black surface. Remembered her mother's face and the love that filled her expression in those final moments. And she knew, in an instant, what she had to do. Seeing the water not as a dark and terrible foe, but as an ally to help save her beloved. As her own mother had done for her. Strength washed through her, her spine straightened and her chin lifted.

As Giovanni took his first step up the scaffolding nearby, she gave a loud cry, drawing the attention of half those assembled, including her own father. She wheeled on her heel, tossing aside her lace handkerchief, and plunged into the frigid canal.

The icy shock hit her, stealing her breath and numbing her limbs. Though it did not matter – she knew not how to swim. Large air bubbles floated to the inky surface. She watched, one by one, as they burst. There was no point in resisting. After all, it would be Giovanni's chance at freedom. Even if she herself could not share it with him, he might be given life. Long moments threaded by, interwoven with short struggles for air she did not heed.

She saw first her father's face, contorted in rage as he ripped apart the canvas that night in the courtyard. But instead of anger, she felt compassion fill her, realizing now she could forgive him. For he had simply been reacting in fear. And fear knew not the sweet refrain of love. Love that was hers and Giovanni's. Her beloved's image floated before her next and her heart swelled, joy coursing through her. She reached out, the illusion dissipating even as she opened her mouth in a futile attempt for oxygen. She felt her lungs strain, and then, strangely, a giddy, almost blissful sensation begin to creep through her. How pleasant, she thought

sleepily.

Giovanni's face appeared once more, wreathed in bubbles, eyes wide. Ah, she thought, what loveliness to have my final vision be of him. She did not reach for him this time, instead drawing comfort from his mere visage. She felt blackness start to edge in.

His features, however, did not fade, but drew nearer. His hands closed around her arms, tugging her back up, up, up, toward light, toward life. With a cry, his head broke the surface, Alessandra's almost-inert body resting on his shoulder.

Conte Velocchi sank to his knees. He stretched out his shaking arms to Alessandra, repeating over and over, "My darling, my baby."

Giovanni swam to the edge, lifting Alessandra up to her father as eager hands helped him out of the freezing waters too.

Rocking his daughter back and forth, the conte kissed her face and stroked her sodden hair, murmuring in her ear.

Someone from the crowd placed a wool blanket around her shoulders. Slowly, slowly, her eyes opened and she blinked, sputtering and coughing. "Father?"

"Shhh, shhhh, it's all over now. All over."

"No, no!" Her eyes widened, her hand clutched at his sleeve, and she shook her head weakly, whispering, "It cannot be."

He smoothed her forehead. "It is not as you think." The conte swallowed. "Giovanni saved your life." Warm drops fell from her father's eyes onto her damp skin. "For that, his own has been spared."

Giovanni came to Alessandra's father, bowing low, placing his hand on his heart. "I owe you my eternal gratitude."

"And you, mine." The conte and the artist regarded each other. But where once there was hatred, now only love remained.

Conte Velocchi looked down into his daughter's eyes. "Darling, darling," he said, his eyes brimming, "I was so wrong." He bowed his head. "Only fear destroys. And I was so afraid, so afraid that love would be my ruination. That you and Givoanni would ruin what I had guarded so long and so hard. What I thought needed to be protected, in fact, needed to be given flight. On wings of love..." Tears choked his throat. "Please," he whispered, voice hoarse. "Please forgive me."

Her eyelids quivered and sobs burst from her. "I do, Father." She wound her arms around his neck, hugging him to her. "I do."

Dawn broke the over the rooftops, flooding the entire square in golden luminance. The light morning breeze caressed the onlookers, a hushed reverence flowing through them.

Without another word, Conte Velocchi let Giovanni scoop Alessandra into his arms. Giovanni cupped Alessandra's face gently, stroking a finger down her cheek, softly kissing her lips. "I love you," he murmured. "And I shall create a hundred more paintings of you and your remarkable deed, to commemorate this day, this moment, and our love."

As the lovers' embrace tightened, dawn's palette brushed the sky a hopeful pink, the light edging everything it touched in pure gold.

"And now I am free," she replied, "to love you forever."

# Acknowledgments

Shannon Page – copyeditor, who had a great eye for detail

Angela Waters – graphic designer, who gave me a beautiful cover for the story

SRW writing group – who helped me keep up my writer morale

# Beside A Moonlit Shore

## A Novelette

*#2 in the Love By Moonlight Series*

# Jessica Eissfeldt

Beside A Moonlit Shore
Jessica Eissfeldt

# Chapter One

MY FINGERS TIGHTENED AROUND THE crumpled telegram and I felt the edges bite into my palm. The errand boy had taken off his hat and bowed his head, and without a word, handed me the black-edged page.

*Charles.* I could hear his name keening on the wind as the sting of sea salt air mixed with the tears that had come, as they always did, sudden and sharp.

Staring out over the cliff's edge, in the moonlight rapidly being covered by dark clouds, I shivered.

September 2. Two years ago, today.

September 2. Also the day he had proposed. And the day we had gotten married. I rubbed my ring finger, twisting the wedding band that was no longer there.

I clenched my fingers into a fist, the knuckles turning white, as white as the

whitecaps now frothing on the steely surface of the open ocean. No safe harbor out there. All souls lost. I trembled as I recalled the typed words.

I swallowed, my right hand coming up to clutch at the gold brooch at my collar—his wedding gift to me. Raindrops now soaked my birds' nest of a hairdo. He'd always called it that, just before he would tumble my black curls loose from their hairpins and kiss my neck. "Oh Charles," I whispered. But the wind ripped even his name away from me.

I closed my eyes, my lashes matting against each other as I took a step forward. The rain fell harder still.

I took another step. Could feel the open expanse of empty air in front of me, envision, even with closed eyes, the weathered and crumbling cliff face with its plunging precipice. The crash of the waves. The sharpness of the rocks.

I held my breath. Pressed one booted toe closer to the edge, the rain continuing to pelt me, hammer me. I'd meant every word of my wedding vows. Every single word.

I brought my other foot squarely beside the first one, into the damp, soft earth. It crumbled beneath me, and with a shriek, I lost my balance. I squeezed my eyes shut. My arms pinwheeled and I pitched backward, the wind keening and shrieking around me.

I pried my eyes open. I was still alive. The wind shrieked and tore at my skirts, my hair, my face. I looked around. The shrieking changed to a yowl. I held my breath. Listened again. The yowl grew more insistent as the rain came in sheets now.

Again the yowl. A cat, I realized. I looked around again, not seeing anything. But as another shriek pierced the storm's howling, I spotted a small ledge a few feet below the outcropping. I stared harder, and saw the tip of what looked like an orange ear just above the rock.

I remembered the low, rumbling purr of my childhood cat, Puff. Saw her soft, curled limbs. Felt her silken fur. Remembered snuggling with her on the settee, feeding her bites of my liver paté.

The meowing continued. I crouched down, and wiped the sting of rainwater out of my eyes.

I felt the toe of my buttoned boot slip. But I couldn't just leave the tiny bit of fluff. The rain-soaked little kitten had not chosen its fate. Unlike me. I tightened my jaw, held my breath. Peered over the ledge.

There, perched mere meters below me, was the tiniest, most bedraggled kitten I'd ever seen. It barely resembled a cat, in fact, for its little body was so drenched in rainwater, and its ears were so flattened to its head, that it had begun to look more like a lump of orange mud than a kitten.

But its yowl remained unmistakable.

Sinking to my knees, I reached my hand down and found I could, if I stretched my arm and fingers to their fullest length, just brush the kitten's front paw. I tried hooking my finger around its front paw but it shrieked again. Was it hurt?

Shifting my weight further forward, bits of soil crumbled away and I dug my fingers in the earth, heart hammering. The kitten mewled. I reached out again. The kitten scooted backward, out of my reach. The rain kept sluicing. Throwing out all propriety, I sank onto my stomach, my silk blouse edged in Irish lace now a sodden mess.

I stretched my arm out again towards the kitten. But it move away. Meowed again. Its tiny mouth showed razor-sharp teeth that did it no good in this fight against nature. My heart squeezed and I inched forward on my belly, the rain still pouring down, my hair almost completely undone, matted around my face and neck.

I felt more soil crumble and fall away into the darkness below. The kitten mewled again. I set my chin. It would not die if I could help it.

I held my breath and moved another inch forward, mindful of the cold nothingness almost directly below me, one hand pressed against the slippery mud, the other now close enough to the kitten that I could pass one finger along its head. But how to scoop it up?

It mewled again and fixed me with its large amber eyes, its expression appearing half-baleful, half-resigned as it squeezed its eyes shut against the near-gale.

Just a half-inch more...

"It's all right, my love," I cooed to the kitten as it tried wriggling from my grasp. But I held firm. I swallowed. There had to be a way. If there was a will, there would

be a way.

Looking around in the rapidly fading light, I spotted the faint gleam of rock, now slick with rain. It would not work with my smooth-soled boots. But if I was barefoot? Without hesitation, I unlaced my boots, removed my stockings and placed them nearby. But the wind picked them up, threw them over the ledge. They made not a sound as they fell. I shuddered.

I wiggled my toes; now I had better grip. And it looked as if the rocks would hold. I wriggled farther, now able to snare the loose skin at the base of the kitten's neck between my thumb and forefinger. But just as I began to pull the kitten up from the rocky outcropping, I felt the edge begin to give way beneath me. Trying to haul myself up while still gripping the kitten, I ground my teeth together.

But the mud seemed to have other ideas. Its slickness allowed my free hand no purchase and the faster I tried to scramble up and backwards, the more soil crumbled away from the sheer drop. I swallowed.

In one quick motion, I brought my arm, with the wriggling animal, up as quickly as

I could. But the swift motion and the kitten's struggling caused me to overbalance, and I swayed back and forth. My fingers scrabbled at nothing, raking the dirt.

I brought the kitten in closer to my chest and squeezed my eyes shut, heart pounding, as I prayed that shifting my weight would make a difference. It did. I rolled away from the cliff face and let out a long, slow breath, clutching the kitten to my chest, its heart pounding just as wildly as mine.

Who knows how long it had been out on that ledge? Hours? Days? I stroked its tiny head and saw its eyes close, but noticed a tiny trickle of blood on its left front paw.

A chill breeze swirled by. No time for dawdling. I still had to get out of here. And now it was almost dark. My eyes darted to the churning waters far below and I felt my stomach drop. I shivered as a gust of wind plastered my skirts to my legs.

Pulling myself to my knees, I swayed slightly before regaining my balance and slowly standing. I took hasty steps away from the edge and back up the path.

# Chapter Two

HUGGED THE KITTEN CLOSE, stroking a finger across its head. I'd saved it from certain death only by my own foolish actions. It didn't even realize that. And it was purring, for heaven's sake.

Purring. The sound grew louder, its whole body vibrating with the happy noise. I felt laughter start in my belly even as tears welled in my eyes.

Purring. I brought its softness to my cheek. A fierce protectiveness stole over me and I hugged the kitten tighter.

Wiping my tears away, I noticed the pus and dried blood on its tiny swollen left front paw. The kitten hissed.

Dr. Shaw. He lived within walking distance of this remote clifftop. He might be able to examine it. If he was home.

I gathered my skirts in my hand, tucked the kitten into my skirt pocket. And ran.

The darkened windows of the doctor's low, yellow house made my heart sink. But I wouldn't give up that easily.

Throwing aside all propriety, I pounded on his front door. Minutes passed. Nothing but the howling of the wind replied. I pounded again, further damaging my soft kidskin gloves. No matter, though. For they were already ruined, streaked with mud and stiff with the dried blood from the kitten's wound.

I readjusted the kitten's position to my left elbow and raised my right hand to knock again when the door flew open and Dr. Shaw appeared in his shirtsleeves, broad shoulders nearly filling the doorway, his dark hair disheveled, his eyes bleary with sleep. But his eyes widened as he saw me.

"Mrs. Hampton? What's wrong? Who's hurt?"

I colored. "I know it is late, but this little beast was half-drowned in the downpour and he's injured, to boot."

He blinked as he took in my own disheveled appearance.

"May I come in?"

"I'm afraid sleep has impaired my judgment and I forget my manners. Please, do come in."

Inclining my head, I stepped across the threshold.

"Now, wherever did you find this poor creature?" He took the kitten but studied me.

As Dr. Shaw's gaze rested on me, something in the way his eyes met mine had me stepping back, examining the mud now caked to my sleeve. I brushed a fallen lock of hair out of my eyes and took a deep breath. What could I say to him? He would wonder why I was out in a rainstorm in the first place.

"I took a walk," I declared.

"I see," he said, turning his attention back to the kitten. "You do know, Mrs. Hampton, that I am not a veterinarian."

I inclined my head. "I am well aware of it."

"But I will see what I can do. For a creature in pain is still a creature in pain, regardless if it be furred, feathered or smooth-skinned."

Such poetics. Rather shocking, coming from a country doctor. I hid my smile. The second one this evening. What had gotten into my head?

As the doctor examined the kitten, my eyes wandered the room, taking in the sparse furnishings, the neat but somewhat threadbare settee in the corner below the bay window. With a view of the water, I realized, blinking back sudden tears, my hands clenching into fists, hidden from sight in the folds of my skirt. I blinked again, managing to contain myself, taking a deep breath once more. Nothing less than expected in a country doctor's home. In a bachelor's home. I felt my cheeks color once more.

I watched Dr. Shaw bandage the kitten's paw with gauze, his long fingers swift and sure, his strong hands gentle and well-practiced.

He looked up at me. "There you are. The little one just needs a bit of rest. Of course, with kittens, I don't guarantee it." He chuckled. "Looks like it got some sort of sticker stuck in its paw. That's why it was swollen and sore. But I extracted the irritant and it should be fine now."

"Thank you, Dr. Shaw," I managed through now-chattering teeth.

He frowned. "Are you all right? Where did you say you found the kitten?"

"On the cliffside."

"In this weather? It's nearly a hurricane out there."

"It was only a gale," I said, doing all I could to stop my teeth from chattering. I rubbed my arms, meeting his gaze. I shivered, suddenly remembering my bare feet and drawing them toward the chair legs, under my skirt. Praying he hadn't noticed that indecency.

"Have something hot to drink, at least. And then I will drive you back home."

"Oh, I couldn't impose at this hour. Please." I stood up. But as I began to sway on my feet, he caught my elbow and helped me back down to the settee.

Coming back a few minutes later with two steaming mugs, he handed me one. Our fingers brushed and I flinched. He had the good grace not to notice. Or so I thought.

I saw a flicker of concern pass over his countenance, his voice low. "How long has it been, Mrs. Hampton?"

Despite everything, my muddy feet, disheveled appearance and ruined gown, I brought my hand to my chest. "I beg your pardon?"

"Please allow me to clarify my statement. Since your husband's passing. How many months has it been since your husband's passing?"

Misinterpreting the horrified expression that continued to appear on my face, he cleared his throat. "Do forgive me. It's simply that, as your physician, I do have some experience in matters of psychology and it seems to me that, if I may be so bold..." He trailed off, looking at me once more. I simply blinked and nodded wearily, suddenly too exhausted to care.

"...that your mental state, shall we say," he chose his words carefully, "is still somewhat...fragile?"

I studied the rim of the chipped ceramic mug and merely nodded, tears again prickling at the back of my eyes.

"I thought as much," he said, his voice now a mere whisper. "And judging from your present appearance, and the lateness of the hour, well, I can only surmise," he cleared his throat, "that things are not going well. That perhaps..." His brown eyes studied me with a mixture of compassion and concern, "you are not happy with...you have not, perhaps... That is to say," he cleared his throat again, "you might still be suffering the strain of loss." His voice tapered off at the last word, as if saying it somehow softly would make it hurt less.

"You...you did not know my late husband."

"I do apologize but—"

"But I should be going," I said between clenched teeth. "Thank you for the tea." I paid great care in setting the mug back down on the sideboard. Just as I stood, the soft tickle of fur brushed against my ankles. "Oh!"

"The kitten." He leaned forward to pick the animal up.

I hoped that my ankles were not visible. Not that propriety mattered anymore. And he was the doctor. But still.

He handed me the kitten.

"Is it a boy or girl?" I asked and straightened, smoothing a stray strand off my forehead, as Dr. Shaw handed me the kitten.

"A boy," he said, as I pressed the kitten to my bodice. It meowed, struggled, wanting down.

"I see. I'd like to take my leave now."

"Very well," Dr. Shaw said. "As you wish. I'd advise you to get some rest. And don't worry about the kitten. They, I've found, have a remarkable ability to heal themselves when left alone to let nature take its course."

"I'll be sure to remember that, Dr. Shaw. Now, I really must be going." I held my head with as much dignity as I could muster, the kitten tucked under my arm.

Dr. Shaw simply nodded and opened the door for me. The wind had scrubbed the sky free of clouds, and now a pale sliver of moon shone in the starry, now-quiet night. I stepped out the door. But then my bare feet hit the cold ground. I jerked back, nearly bumping into the doctor.

He placed a warm hand on my chilled arm.

"Oh!" I turned slowly, a blush flaming on my cheeks. I averted eye contact with him until I could no longer. "I do believe," my voice came out in a whisper, as I raised my gaze to his, "I would like to accept your kind offer of transportation."

# Chapter Three

THE LAST ECHO OF HOOFBEATS faded
away as Dr. Shaw's buggy pulled
away from the door. I sighed. And
shivered. I had to get out of these wet
things. And, I thought as I looked down at
the kitten, give this one something to eat.

I combed through the snarls in my hair
while seated on the quilt on my bed,
watching the kitten across the room
lapping up a saucer of milk. I could hear his
purring as if he were right beside me.

Charles was always talking about cats
being good luck on ships. I slipped into a
warm high-necked nightgown with eyelet
embroidered on its collar and cuffs. The
wrought iron bedframe creaked under my
weight as I sat back down and began
plaiting my hair. My eyes strayed to the
kitten, who was now giving himself a bath.

That's what I had been running from.

My fingers stilled. From thoughts of Charles as if they were his ghost, hanging specter-like in my mind. The kitten clambered up and then across the pale lavender double-wedding-ring quilt, onto my lap, and then curled up in a ball right in the middle of my pillow. I tied the ribbon around the end of my braid, blew out the lantern and lay down.

As my head sank into the feather pillow, the kitten's purring was the last thing I heard before I fell asleep.

A BRISK BREEZE AND A sky still scrubbed free of clouds greeted me upon awakening the following morning. I blinked and yawned. But before I could move, a set of tiny claws buried themselves in the quilt around my feet. Laughter bubbled up inside me, then spilled out and into the quiet of the morning. And, my, how good it felt.

"Ouch!" I said, leaning down and gently extracting the kitten's claws from my feet. "I'm beginning to think I shall call you Purr. That's all you do, it seems." I laid my

cheek against its soft fur and closed my eyes, feeling his rumbling vibrations.

"So you're a boy," I addressed the kitten, setting him carefully back on the quilt, remembering what Dr. Shaw had said.

Dr. Shaw. The memory of his words came back to me, along with his warm but concerned brown eyes, and I felt my hands tremble.

Societal expectations dictated a year's worth of mourning. Charles had been gone exactly that long. No. It took time. It took time. And yet. And yet, a tiny voice whispered in my ear, how much longer was I going to hold on to a ghost?

Besides, today was my first day back in the schoolroom after the summer. My students were counting on me. No amount of tears would bring Charles back into my arms.

Crying mottled my complexion anyway. I made a wry face at the kitten, who simply blinked and yawned, his pink mouth opening and shutting so quickly you couldn't quite see the flash of danger. But yet it lingered.

Just like fear, I realized. Just like fear. There was no stopping it. But I could choose to be stronger than the fear. I stood up, placing the kitten gently on the bed before splashing cold water on my face in the rose-patterened wash basin and then drawing on a fresh skirt and blouse. It felt like a fresh opportunity. Yesterday's clothes; yesterday's fears, I mused. Both would have to be thrown straight out.

After gathering my books for the day, I poured a saucer of milk for the kitten, closed the front door and set off for the schoolhouse.

# Chapter Four

AFTER SCHOOL THAT AFTERNOON, I put the canvas bag of books on the side table and took a step forward, nearly tripping over the ball of fluff that had somehow gotten under my feet. The kitten.

I swooped down and picked him up, burying my face in his fur. As they always had this time of year, the schoolchildren had clammered for sea tales. And I'd put them off yet again.

I swallowed, glancing up at the narrow attic stairs.

The stairs creaked under my weight as I climbed the narrow passage to the third floor. Flinging open the trapdoor, I sneezed as dust motes danced on a stray sunbeam. My, but how much dust could accumulate in two years' time. My eyes flitted to the sole object in the room.

His sea chest. Gingerly, I walked over to it, its navy blue paint just as shiny as the day he'd brought it home. Each brass rivet polished. Ship shape, I could almost hear his voice whisper those words, with his half smile and that sparkle in his eyes. I felt my throat tighten. Placing a single fingertip on its smooth, cool surface, I let the coolness soothe me. Wash me. Bathe me in its calming solidarity. The knot in my throat loosened enough for me to open my eyes and slowly, slowly, lift the lid.

Sandalwood and cinnamon. His scent. I snatched my hands back as if burned. The lid crashed shut. I jumped. Immediately a thousand memories flooded me. Us laughing in the sunshine. The way his hair ruffled in the wind right before he set sail. The feel of his hand along my skin. The exact shade of his eyes—somewhere between cerulean and aquamarine with just the slightest tint of sea-foam green. I felt tears seep between the fingers I had pressed to my face, the arms I had wrapped around myself, pretending even for a moment that they were of his embrace. His touch. His essence.

His essence. The thought stopped the

shaking of my shoulders, lessened the flow of damp heat from my eyes. That was it. I lifted my head. Took a deep breath and lifted the chest's lid again. Inhaled slowly—tenderly, delicately, as if each tiny particle contained his true self. As if, in those moments, I could reach out and almost, almost touch him. But I could, I realized with wonder.

I set my hand on the first object stowed neatly on top. Felt the stiff starching of the linen bag protecting that very first present he'd brought back to me. From India, he'd said. And then regaled me with a tale of how the Raj had personally comissioned its carving.

Tiny ivory roses in a tiny jewelry box. Yes, I could feel it through the bag. Untying the cords, the heart-shaped box sat in the center of my palm. I could feel its solidness. Its weight. And as my fingers gently closed around the token of love he'd brought from so far away, I felt the memory of his love surround me, as well.

Felt his heart and soul pour through me, as if he was right there. Standing in that very room holding me, his arms around me, his face buried in my hair. And we were laughing. Laughing just like the day we were first married. Just like that very first day so full of hope and promise and everything beautiful. Magical. Wonderful. I felt the tears pool at my feet.

As if everything....

I could feel how much he loved me. How much he loved me still. Even now. Even after he'd been gone so very long. How could I go on without him?

But as his love continued to radiate through me, like diamond shards of light, emanating, it seemed, from the box, I felt the tears give way to a peculiar form of joy. Hope, even. Joy that he was not, in fact, lost, but joy that he would always be forever alive. Inside me.

Inside my heart and soul.

In a place that would always be accessible to me. He had not left. And he never would as long as I breathed. I could tuck that special place away, carry that spot within my heart for him, and him alone. And it would always be there. Always. I felt a swirling inside of me as the hopeful green shoots of renewal began to unfurl themselves. It didn't make it wrong to love again. In fact, he would have wanted me to

be happy. I felt the diamond shards of light glow, glitter and then gently, slowly, begin to fade one by one like the final stars fading out before the dawn.

But instead of alarm, I simply felt warm, placing a hand on my heart, closing my eyes, remembering. Remembering that space inside of me. And then I smiled.

Taking a deep, steadying breath, I began unwrapping the rest of those precious objects. So many trips. So many times he'd come back to me with love in his heart and a beautiful gift for me. So many things we'd shared—good and bad.

My hand glided across the sleek surface of a teak telescope, recalling the nor'easter tale he'd spun upon presenting me with the glass.

I next found the delicately arranged sails of a ship in a bottle. Smiled as I remembered him telling me it was a scale replica of Blackbeard's ship. And that roguish glint in his eyes when he'd said there was a reason his middle name was Morgan. Pirates in the blood. That's why he'd become a sea captain, after all. All up and down the Eastern Seaboard, he'd said, his ancestors had sailed.

Drawing the treasures out, I gently blew off the dust and set them in that patch of sunshine. Turning back to the sea chest, I reached into its depths, my hands closing around a fat leather-bound volume, when I felt something land on my foot.

"Oh!" I turned my head. The kitten. But as fast as he'd landed, he jumped away, landing on an invisible enemy in the pool of sunshine, spinning around and around as he tried to capture his tail.

A laugh escaped me as I watched him, his concentration so intense, so in the moment that it left no room for doubt or worry or fear. He was simply right here. Right now. Perhaps, if a kitten could do it, so could I. I caught my breath.

Yes.

And now he was vigorously licking a spot on his back, craning his head around, his pink tongue diligent. My smile grew wider and wider until it turned into another laugh.

My merriment flowed outward, seeking an outlet from the place that it had been locked up in for so long, from the prison of grief that I had trapped it in. Kept from air and light and sunshine.

I took a deep breath through my laughter, tears of mirth now streaming down my face. I put a hand up to my face, the wetness transferring onto my fingers.

My hand came to rest on the orange fur of the kitten, who now had finished his ever-so-urgent bath and was curled up in a ball, fitting perfectly into that spot of sunshine on the floorboards, his side rising and falling. A faint purr emanated from him—I could feel its vibration through my palm.

What would I have done had he not been there? He had saved my life, I realized, even more than I had saved his. For if he had not been there, I would have continued my descent into darkness.

I continued stroking his fur. For his role as savior in my darkest hour, I realized, he needed some recognition of his own. I would bring him to the schoolroom tomorrow.

The children would love that.

And these treasures? What good were they up here, shut away in blackness when they deserved to see the light of day? To be admired. Cherished. Loved. I placed a hand gently on the leather-bound volume. Just as Charles had loved me, these objects deserved love as well. They would go to school too.

Scooping up the kitten, I took a final look around the attic before going downstairs, pulling the trapdoor firmly shut.

# Chapter Five

"Now Bobby," I turned to a red-haired boy on the first bench, "you may go first."

He blushed to the roots of his hair but straightened his shirt and began his speech, then hurried back to his seat.

After every pupil had spoken, I stood and raised my chin. "I've got a surprise for you. I've brought something of my own for show and tell."

I took the ship in a bottle out of my canvas bag, the slight tremble in my fingers the only betrayal of my outward calm. I set the bottle down ever so gently, careful not to jostle the tiny sails. Eyes wide with wonder, the smallest boy seated on the front bench leaned forward so far he toppled over, causing a ripple of laughter from half the schoolroom. I silenced them with a look.

"This was my..." I cleared my throat. Started again. "Can anyone tell me what this is?"

Hands raised. Cries of "it's a ship" and "it's a bottle" ensued.

I nodded. "You're both right. This is a ship in a bottle. It takes years and years and years to make. Sea captains—" I felt a slight prick at the back of my eyes, which I blinked away. "Sea captains," I continued, my voice stronger, "make these. When they come home from a far-off voyage, they come home to the people they love and the land they treasure. Because these objects are far more than simple objects. They represent a connection with the heart and soul of the ocean."

I turned back to my canvas bag. Reached in. "The trials and tribulations of all that a sea captain's life entails. Because of that connection the seamen have with the waves, the salt water, the rhythms and undulations of each and every droplet of water, these objects become a part of the sea captain himself. The compass." I held it up, the gold sparkling in the afternoon light.

"And the sextant." I lifted my other

hand. "Two tools of navigation that a captain could never do without. He, in fact, owes his very existence on the ocean to these objects. And of course, to the stars that guide him, twinkling in that vast inky blackness." As my voice grew stronger, I could almost feel Charles there with me, standing just behind me, supporting me and giving me the words I was looking for, passing along his love of the sea to all these fresh faces. I smiled as once again I felt enveloped by his love as I stroked a finger over the solid brass of the compass.

"Now," I said, "who would like to see these first?"

A sea of hands raised.

"Wonderful. Let's line up, youngest to eldest." I looked around the room as the pupils began to rearrange themselves. "Stand quietly," I added. "And I shall go and get your second surprise now that you're all done with your studies."

Leaving the schoolroom, I turned my face to the breeze, tasting the salty air, its tang skimming over me and stirring the tendrils that had escaped my bun. It felt like a caress. Like Charles. I placed a hand against my own cheek, smiling, letting out a long, deep sigh. Oh, how good it felt to finally let this go. To finally share the delights and wonders of the seafaring life. I was honoring him. Making peace with his passing. And with myself.

I reached down and picked up the wicker basket, returning to the schoolroom doorway with it on my arm.

The kitten's orange head popped over the edge of the basket and shrieks of delight filled the room when the littlest children saw him. They jumped up and ran to where I was standing.

"Can we pet him? Oh can we? Can we? Please, please please?" The little girls leaned in.

I smiled. "Of course. Why don't you go shut the door and we can let him play with his favorite toy that I brought."

I took a step back, surveying the room. The little and big girls crowded around the kitten while the older and younger boys crowded around Charles' treasures. I watched the kitten batting at a piece of red yarn, and watched the boys play with the spyglass and sextant. I felt my shoulders relax and my heart expand.

After a few more minutes, I clapped

my hands together. "All right, boys and girls, class is dismissed. It's time to go home."

Exclamations of surprise and disappointment filled the air—with more gusto than I'd heard before. Everyone gathered up books and supplies and filed out the door. Everyone, that is, except Bobby.

I saw him sitting on his bench, holding the spyglass on his lap, legs swinging absently, his eyes downcast. Were those tears I saw him wipe away with a furtive fist?

Getting up from my desk, I crouched down beside him.

His voice came out barely above a whisper. "My d-daddy..." I saw his lip tremble once again. "Told me he was gonna get me a present like this for m-my b-b-birthday." He stopped. Looked up at me. Unable to control his lip trembling any more, he burst into tears. "But he went away and n-n-never c-came back... Mama," he gasped for air, "Mama said it's cuz he got sick and had to go away to a san-a...san-a-tar-a...something, but I know it's cuz he doesn't..." his voice lowered to a bare whisper, "*love* me." And he threw himself into my arms.

Wrapping my arms around his shaking body, I held him until his sobs subsided. Then I drew my handkerchief out of my pocket and wiped at his face gently, watching his fat fingers clutch the spyglass as if it were a lifeline directly to his father.

"All right, Bobby," I said, my own voice thick, "it's yours. And you know, your father, I'm sure, does love you."

With trembling lips, I smiled down at his awed expression, giving him another hug. "Yes," I whispered, as I watched his entire form change from sorrow to jubilance in seconds. "Take good care of it now."

"Oh," he said, his eyes shining as brightly as the brass fittings on the instrument, "I will. Forever and always."

"You do that, Bobby. You do that," I whispered after him, dabbing my handkerchief to my eyes.

Crossing back to my desk to gather my book bag, I slipped the remaining treasures back into the pouch I'd so carefully wrapped them in and felt contentment settling over me like a warm shawl. Suddenly I felt lighter than air. Scooping up the kitten, who had been chasing his tail

in dizzy circles underneath a desk, I tucked him into the book bag and stepped outside, pulling the schoolhouse door shut.

I stepped off the schoolhouse stoop.

"Mrs. Hampton."

"Doctor Shaw. Good afternoon."

"Good afternoon." He lifted his hat.

I felt my stomach surge with a sudden flutter of butterflies.

Then I saw the bouquet of Black-Eyed Susans in his hand and felt a blush creep up my neck. How did he know Black-Eyed Susans were my favorite?

"I've come to apologize." His gaze fell to the ground and his rather scuffed boots.

"Oh?"

"Yes. I'm afraid my behavior the other evening was somewhat...uncalled for. And for that, I profusely apologize."

I stared for what felt like a full minute at the flowers, wondering yet again how he could have known that that type of daisy was my favorite.

Unless...I swallowed, taking a deep breath. And then I blinked. For the only way he could've realized I loved that type of flower was because he saw me bring a bouquet of them every week to the spot on the hillside cemetery. The path to the cemetery that wound past his house.

I caught my breath. He must have known all this time as well. All...this...time...

Not knowing what else to say, I silently reached a hand out. And accepted the flowers. Accepted his apology. And accepted his attentions.

I smiled up into his warm brown eyes—so different than Charles' blue ones. I studied the outline of Dr. Shaw's face—the smooth skin, a stark contrast to the tanned, weather-lined face of my former husband.

And in that moment, even though his appearance might be worlds apart from Charles', I knew that in their hearts, they were the same—good men.

So I simply took the bouquet. And the arm that he offered. I smiled up at him. "Yes, let's go."

## Thanks for reading! Want more sweet romance?

Turn the page to meet Belinda Thompson in *Dialing Dreams.*

It's the first in my Sweethearts & Jazz Nights series set in 1940s San Francisco.

## *FOR A LIMITED TIME*
## GET YOUR FREE SWEET ROMANCE HERE!

Get your free copy of the sweet romance *Dialing Dreams*, the first in my Sweethearts & Jazz Nights series. Normally my stories are $2.99 and up, but this one is yours FREE when you download it at your favourite online retailer.

*Belinda Thompson, a telephone operator, longs to sing in the spotlight. But when Belinda puts through a fateful midnight call for Nick Hart, a broken-hearted jazz crooner who offers her a chance at her dream, will theirs be only a switchboard connection or something more, in the City by the Bay?*

## Go here to get started:

www.books2read.com/dialingdreams

## *FOR A LIMITED TIME*

Now, read on for an excerpt from Belinda Thompson's story,

*Dialing Dreams:*
*Sweethearts & Jazz Nights, #1*

# Chapter One

BELINDA THOMPSON COULDN'T STAND ONE more moment of this. What was she doing here anyway, sitting at a switchboard at midnight, humming jazz melodies to herself? Melodies that she'd practiced through all four years of high school vocal classes. And then sang for hours more in the kitchen at home, with her heart full of hope and dreams. So shouldn't she be enchanting audiences and singing songs, not answering calls and connecting wires?

But the sound of her father's hoarse cough echoed through her mind and tugged at her conscience. She would not abandon him. She straightened up. She was all he had. She might not want to work as a telephone operator at the Hotel Whitcomb but she could still choose how she acted about it. She would do it—for him. Taking comfort in that, she began the jazz tune again. But it faded from her lips when a call came in.

"Operator. How may I transfer your call?" She cringed as a male voice slurred a greeting.

"No...no tra-transfer. Please, can we just...talk?"

Not only drunk, he's desperate, she thought. Yet his velvety baritone intrigued Belinda in spite of herself. "I'm sorry, sir. You have to tell me who you want to connect to."

"Room five oh...five. Yeah, that's it."

Belinda studied the tips of her polished nails. "One moment, please, while I—"

"No, no, no. No. No...need. I don't...*actually* want to talk to her."

"Sir, who *do* you want to be connected to?"

"There isn't a number. I want...to talk to someone like you."

"I need to connect you. Or I really can't continue this conversation."

"Operator, you sound like a nice girl, and I...need to talk to a nice girl. Claire wasn't—"

A little unnerved, she spoke over him.

"That's not my job."

"All right. All right. I...won't bother...you."

The line went dead.

Belinda frowned then shrugged. She glanced at the clock. Time to go. She collected her purse and slid on her trench coat before cinching its belt. She pinned her hat in place and pulled on her gloves before locking up the tiny switchboard office on the hotel's main floor. With a sigh of relief, she walked through the marble-floored lobby, waved a goodbye to the doorman and headed up Market Street, her seven-cent fare in hand. The cable car's rumble and screech told her she'd arrived just in time to jump onto the Powell-Hyde line and head for home.

*    *    *

A LIGHT DRIZZLE SPATTERED THE phone booth the following Friday night as Nick Hart ducked into it on impulse. Couldn't sleep anyway. And a walk usually cleared his head. He stared out into the darkness enshrouding the Bay Area as the lights of San Francisco winked back at him, as they did every evening across from his place on the waterfront.

Not so long ago, things were going great. His third record was selling well, and he'd gotten his polished shoes onto the crooner stage at last. But this whole thing with Claire had begun to fall apart. He frowned and shook off the raindrops that clung to his fedora, placed it back on his head, and tugged the brim lower.

Eying the sleek black handset, he ran a finger along it as he pondered last week's drunken call to the Hotel Whitcomb. Was he that desperate that he'd actually tried to get sympathy from the operator? Even though she'd been annoyed with him—he hadn't been too drunk to remember that— he couldn't quite forget her satiny voice.

**TURN THE PAGE FOR YOUR EXCLUSIVE BONUS CONTENT!**

**Meet the hero of *Beneath A Venetian Moon,* Givoanni Capriccio. PLUS! Meet the men of my Sweethearts & Jazz Nights series, set in 1940s San Francisco**

**Meet Giovanni Capriccio: the hero of
*Beneath A Venetian Moon, Love By
Moonlight #1***

**Jessica Eissfeldt:** "Tell me about yourself,
Giovanni."

**Giovanni Capriccio:** "What would you
care to know?"

**Jessica:** "Everything. I want to know
everything. But I also want to know why.
Why are you really running? What are you
running from? What caused you to come
to Venice? What are you running away
from? Where is your home, your family?
What is, in essence, your life story?"

**Giovanni:** "Ah, yes, my heritage. My
family. You see," he looked at me, eyes
intense. "I've always felt that drive, that
desire to be an artist, to be a painter, to
create things. When I was little, I was

always drawing. During my lessons, during dinner, during the daytime, the night time. Any time, in truth. I did not stop to think. I only drew. I grew in talent and skill. People began to notice what I was drawing. I drew pictures of friends, of family members. And my rich uncle displayed my painting, one I had done of him, in his hallway. One day, a member of the clergy came to visit and saw the painting. So taken with it, he realized whoever had painted it would be perfect to do a fresco in the refectory hall of my tiny hometown church. So I did that. And word of my talent spread from my town to another town. And another. Until the whole region was commissioning me to do paintings.

### *Sweethearts & Jazz Nights Series*

### **Meet Nick Hart: the hero of *Dialing Dreams, Sweethearts & Jazz Nights #1***

**Jessica Eissfeldt:** "So, Nick, how'd you get to San Francisco?"

**Nick Hart:** "Like I said, my gal left me. Claire." Nick leans back in his chair, pushing the brim of his fedora up higher on his forehead. "She was the one who had brought me to this fine city in the first place. Persuaded me to stick around even though I'd been off to Vegas all the time. We got bitter with each other. We started fighting. She accused me of all sorts of things I didn't do."

Jessica: "Okay. Go on."

Nick: "Got a bit broken-hearted. Wanted sympathy. So I found the only person I thought would listen. The operator."

Jessica: "They do a lot of listening, that's for sure."

Nick: "Didn't figure on falling for her, though." He ran a hand through his hair. "So yeah, I came to San Francisco because of Claire. But I stayed because of Belinda."

**Meet Joe Lucitano: the hero of *Shattered Melodies: Sweethearts & Jazz Nights #2***

**Jessica Eissfeldt:** "So, Joe, what can you tell me about yourself."

**Joe Lucitano:** "Let's see...." He tips the

brim of his hat up. "Well, I was born on a farm outside of the city here – San Francisco – we raised hogs. Not exactly an auspicious beginning." He laughs. "But I always had a hankering for what was new, what was happening; I didn't know much else that kept me entertained than that saxophone of mine."

**Jessica:** "That's great! And you met Claire in school, too, right?"

**Joe:** He nods. "I went to school in San Francisco and that's when I met Claire. In the third grade. She'd just moved to town and looked so cute in that blue sailor suit of hers with the wide collar and the silver buttons."

**Meet Henry Parker: the hero of *Fancy Footwork, Sweethearts & Jazz Nights #3***

**Jessica Eissfeldt:** "Henry, what can you tell me about yourself?"

**Henry Parker:** "I went to Harvard and I studied business. Came in handy when I started to work for Golden Gate Records, 6 years ago. So I've known DuPont – my boss – quite awhile. But where was I? I was born here in San Francisco and raised here, too. This is my town."

**Jessica:** "Right. So what else do you want to tell me?"

**Henry:** "I love jazz and I love to swing dance. I got a job at Golden Gate Records, which was as close to music and jazz that I could get. See, jazz gave me that outlet. I could be free, in listening to it, dancing swing numbers. You just grab a partner and get out on the dance floor."

### Meet Tristan Lavaliere: the hero of *Unspoken Lyrics, Sweethearts & Jazz Nights #4*

**Jessica Eissfeldt:** "So Tristan, tell me about yourself."

**Tristan Lavaliere:** "I love to cook, especially jambalaya and Creole foods that my grandma taught me how to make. She's dead now, though. They're all dead." He frowns and looks out the window. "That's why I took to jazz music after my folks died. It kept me distracted from these thoughts in my head that torment me....Those thoughts keep circling round in my head even as I try to move past it with the music."

**Jessica:** "So you have gotten past it? It's working?"

**Tristan:** "But that's not working!" He shoves a fistful of sheet music off the piano and it flutters onto the floor in a tangled heap. He rakes his hands through his curly, unruly hair and then leans against the window casing, his forearms strong and supply, his smooth skin gilded in the light of dawn. He shakes his head. "So I grew up here on this plantation. It was where I was born and raised." He gives a lopsided smile and I see the dimple on his cheek. "I love the South. And I love where I live. And I love my piano music."

# Acknowledgments

Shannon Page – copyeditor, who had a great eye for detail

Angela Waters – graphic designer, who gave me a beautiful cover for the story

SRW writing group – who helped me keep up my writer morale